BO RABBIT
SMART FOR TRUE
Tall Tales from the Gullah

BO RABBIT
SMART FOR TRUE
Tall Tales from the Gullah

Retold by PRISCILLA JAQUITH

Drawings by ED YOUNG

Philomel Books · New York

Revised edition published in 1995 by Philomel Books, a division of
The Putnam & Grosset Group, 200 Madison Avenue, New York, NY 10016.
Philomel Books, Reg. U.S. Pat. & Tm. Off.
Original edition published in 1981
Published simultaneously in Canada
Lettering by David Gatti
Book designed by Nanette Stevenson and Donna Mark
Text set in New Baskerville

Library of Congress Cataloging-in-Publication Data
Jaquith, Priscilla. Bo Rabbit smart for true: tall tales from the Gullah /
retold by Priscilla Jaquith; drawings by Ed Young.   p.   cm.
These tales were recorded in 1949 for the Library of Congress,
which in 1955 issued a phonodisc under the title: Animal tales told in
the Gullah dialect by Albert H. Stoddard of Savannah, Georgia,
edited by D. B. M. Emrich. Includes bibliographical references.
Contents: Bo Rabbit smart for true—Alligator's Sunday suit—
Cooter's wing—Bo Rabbit's hide-and-seek—Manners for true—Rattlesnake's word.
1. Afro-Americans—Georgia—Folklore.   2. Tales—Georgia.
[1. Folklore, Afro-American.   2. Folklore—Georgia.   3. Folklore—United States.]
I. Young, Ed, ill.   II. Emrich, Duncan, 1908–. comp.
Animal tales told in the Gullah dialect by Albert H. Stoddard of Savannah, Georgia.
III. Stoddard, Albert Henry, 1872–1954.   IV. Title.
PZ8.1.J35Bo   1995   398.2′452′08996073—dc20   93-50596 CIP AC
ISBN 0-399-22668-0
1   3   5   7   9   10   8   6   4   2
First Impression

Printed in Singapore

Contents

For my daughter, Carol J. Patton, with much love

P.J.

From the Author

Stand on the coasts of Georgia and South Carolina and look across the wide water. You'll see lots of little islands—the Sea Islands. Years ago they were covered with rice and cotton, and the men who owned them brought people from Africa to tend the crops.

Nobody knows exactly what part of Africa these people came from. Some scholars say Angola—which is why they are called Gullahs. Others say they came from a tribe in Liberia called the Golas, who spoke so rapidly and oddly that the Dutch called them "Qua Quas," because they sounded like geese gabbling.

The Gullahs came from Africa either directly or by way of the Bahamas and West Indies, and started working on the Sea Island plantations. After the Civil War freed them, they stayed on, amid the ruins of great plantations, hunting and fishing for a living. It wasn't hard. They lived in one of the greatest bird and game lands of America—pinewoods, tidal marshes, broom sedge fields. They hunted until they knew everything about the alligator, deer, fox, rabbit, partridge, and other creatures that lived there. At night, around their cabin fires, they told stories about them, putting these creatures from their new land into tales brought from their African homeland.

Listen to their talk, and it sounds a little like calypso. They mix words from Africa (like "cooter," for "tortoise," from an African word, *kuta*) with Elizabethan English and bits of dialect from Dorset, Devon, and other British provinces (like "bittles" for "victuals").

Many scholars have studied Gullah. Some, like Guy B. Johnson, think the language can be traced back to English dialects spoken by bond servants who worked alongside the Gullahs. Others believe Gullah comes from African languages such as Ewe, Fante, Wolof, and Yoruba.

If someone said to you, "Oonah konnou oonah?" what would you think it meant? Those are actual words recorded in a court trial about the collision of two sailboats. They mean: "Whose boat is that?"

You can forget all about English grammar and spelling when you use Gullah. It has its own vocabulary, takes every possible shortcut, and uses its own syntax and grammar. The same noun can be both singular and plural; the same verb both past and present. For example, "e" is used for "he," "she," or "it." "Shum" is a shortcut for "see" or "saw," "him," "her," "it," or "them." So from two words, "E shum," you can get twenty-four possible sentences.

In addition, words in Gullah can have meanings quite different from other dialects. When Crane tries to sip soup from a flat saucer with his long bill, the Gullahs say his mouth can't "specify"—meaning it doesn't work. And as a swift query, somewhat like the French *n'est-ce pas?*, the Gullahs sprinkle their talk with "enty?"

Many people have tried to write down this special language. One of these was Albert H. Stoddard, who was born in 1872 on his father's plantation on Daufuskie Island, off South Carolina's coast. As a boy he played with Gullah children and learned their language and stories. He grew up and went away to college; when he returned, he wrote down their stories in Gullah. Years later, when he was 77 years old, he asked the Library of Congress if they would like him to record the stories exactly as he had learned them as a child. The library was delighted.

The tales in this book are based on Stoddard's work. You couldn't understand them if they were told as he told them in exact Gullah. But from this version you can get at least an idea of their flavor and humor.

Today some Gullahs still live in wild parts of the Sea Islands. Others have left to work in mainland cities. One of their islands, Hilton Head, has become a playground for the rich, with luxury hotels, big houses, beautiful beaches, and fine golf courses. If you want to read more about the Gullahs, you can find a list of articles and books about them at the end of this book.

–Priscilla Jaquith

BO RABBIT
SMART FOR TRUE

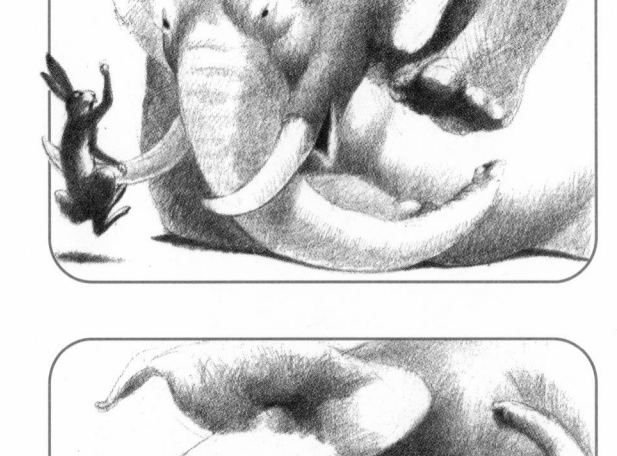

One morning at first-day, Elephant was just lying down in his bed on the high hill when...

"Wait, Elephant! Wait!" cries a voice under his right leg.

Elephant holds his leg heist in the air. "Who's that?"

"It's me." Bo Rabbit hops out. "Why don't you watch what you do, Elephant? You almost mash me."

"You're too little," grumbles Elephant. "Nobody can see you."

"Little! I'm not too little. You're too big. You're one big man, Elephant." He watches Elephant stretch out in his bed. "You're even more big lying down than standing up."

"I know. I'm the biggest thing on earth, Bo Rabbit."

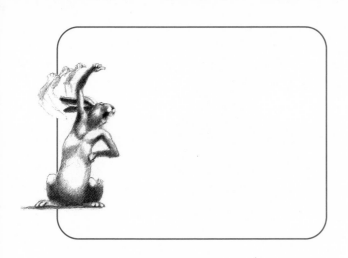

"Elephant, you know one thing? If I wanted to, big as you are and little as I am, I could pull you right out your bed."

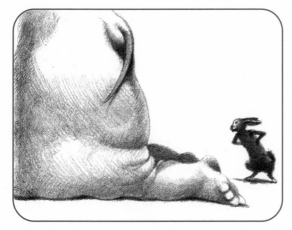

"What kind of talk you talking, Rabbit? I'm up all night. I come here for catch some sleep and you have to come botheration me about pull me out my bed. Go 'long and let me sleep."

"Elephant, if I'm nigh you so your bigness scares me, I can't do it, for true. But if you let me tie one rope to you and get back in the brush where I can't see you, I bet I can pull you right out your bed."

"You couldn't move one of my ears, Rabbit."

"But if I do, Elephant, if I do, you never say I'm too little then, isn't it so?"

"All right, all right. Go away now."

Bo Rabbit takes his departure. He walks on and walks on, *kapot, kapot, kapot,* through the brush and down the hill till he reaches the ocean shore.

Far out in the blue, he sees Whale swimming.

"Hi there, Whale," he hollers.

Whale spouts, *Szi, Szi, Szi,* and leaps high to look towards shore. Then he swims close and pulls up with a great swish of his tail, SPASHOW.

"G'morning, Bo Rabbit."

"Where you been, Whale? I ain't seen you in a long time."

"I been clean around the earth, Rabbit."

"Gracious, Whale, you sure do grow to be one big man."

"I know. I'm the biggest thing in the water, Rabbit."

"Whale, you know one thing?"

"What, Bo Rabbit?"

"Little as I am and big as you are, if I wanted to, I could pull you right out the Salt."

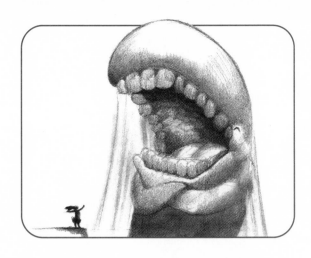

Whale laughs till he sputters, *Shuplu, shuplu, shuplu.* "What kind of talk you talking, Rabbit? You couldn't *move* me in the ocean, let alone pull me out."

"If I'm there when you come out the water so your bigness scares me, I can't do it, for true.

"But if you let me tie one rope to you so I can go back on the hill where I can't see you, I bet I can pull you right out the sea."

"All right, all right. I like to see that, Rabbit. I surely would."

Bo Rabbit goes home and gets a long rope. Then he takes his foot in his hand and runs to Elephant's house.

Elephant is in his bed asleep. Bo Rabbit yells, "Roll over, Elephant. Roll over."

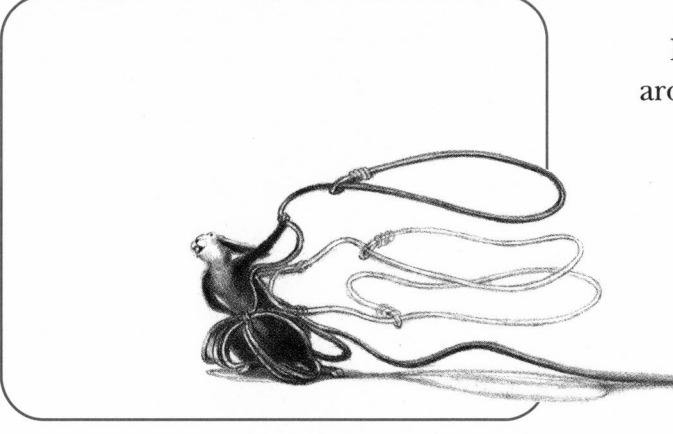

Elephant stirs. Bo Rabbit slings the rope around him in one big loop.

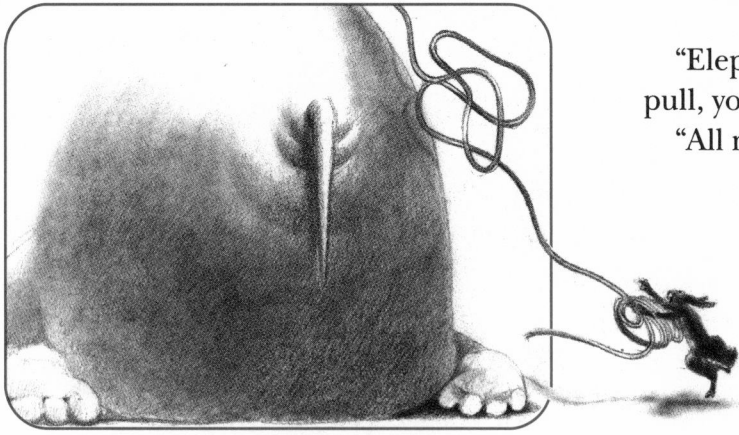

"Elephant," he hollers, "when you feel me pull, you pull hard as you can, hear?"

"All right." Elephant goes back to sleep.

Bo Rabbit takes the other end of the rope and runs down hill to the shore where Whale is waiting.

"Hey, Whale, come close as you can, will you? I like to tie this rope around you."

Whale comes close and Bo Rabbit ties the knot tight.

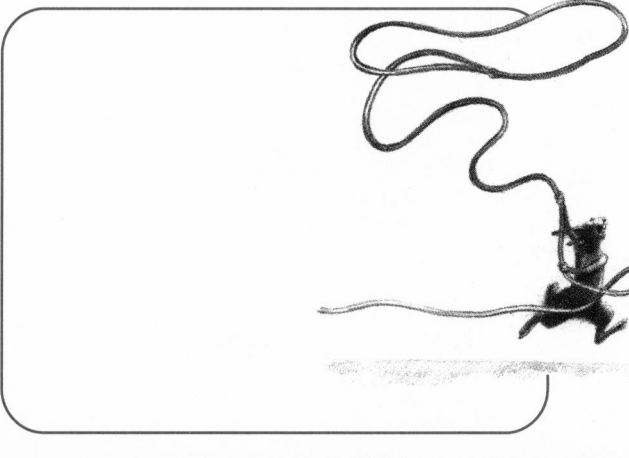

"Whale, when you feel me pull, you pull hard as you can, hear?"

"All right, Rabbit."

Bo Rabbit goes in the middle of the rope and he takes it in all two his hands.

He pulls from all two ends one time, *hrup, hrup, hrup.*

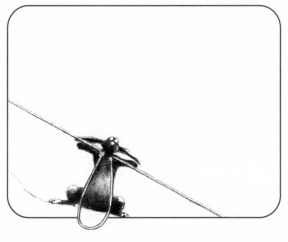

Elephant, asleep in his bed, doesn't have Bo Rabbit in the back part of his head, but Whale is waiting in the water for see what Bo Rabbit will do.

When he feels Bo Rabbit make his pull, he gives a big jerk, KPUT.

The first thing Elephant knows, he's jerked out his bed and goes sumbleset down the hill, *Fahlip, fahlip, fahlip.*

He can't get on his foot. When he does, he starts to pull, *hrup, hrup, hrup.* But all he can pull, he keeps going to the sea.

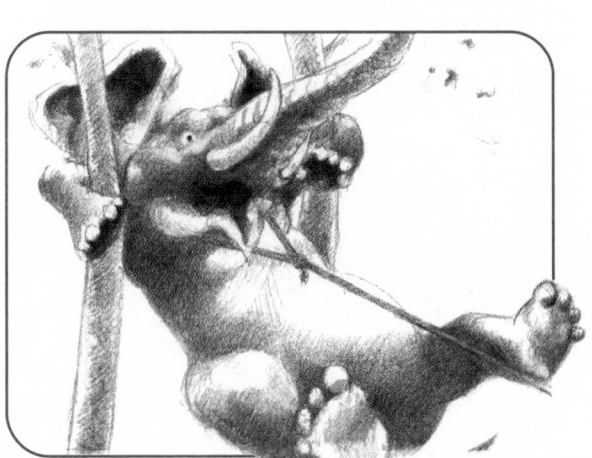

Except he sees two trees and brace himself against them, Whale would have pulled him clean into the sea and drowned him.

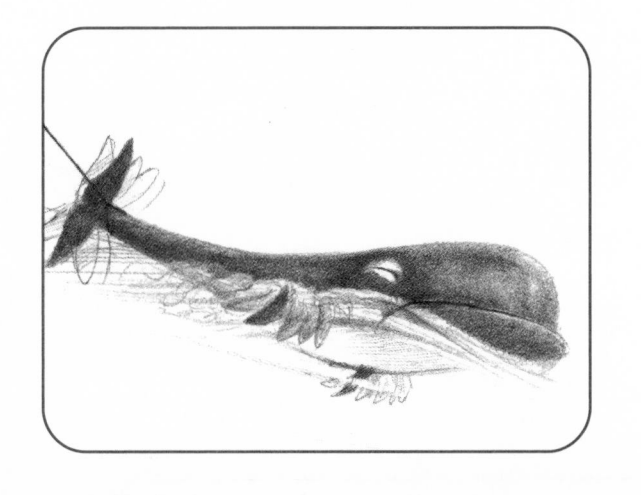

But all Whale pull, *hrup, hrup, hrup,* he can't pull Elephant out of those trees.

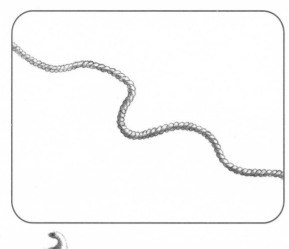

By and by in the sun-hot, Whale gets tired. He gives slack back on the rope and

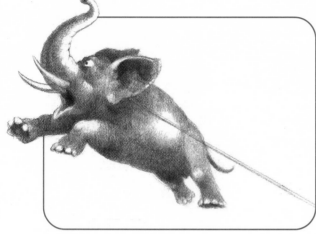

Elephant takes that slack up the hill and pulls Whale clean out of the deep.

Except Whale hold on to a rock in the Salt, Elephant would have pulled him all the way to the high hill.

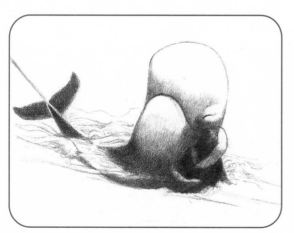

But hard as Elephant pull, *hrup, hrup, hrup,* he can't pull Whale out of the sea.

By and by in the sun-hot, Elephant gets tired. He gives back slack. Whale gives a jerk, KPUT, and pulls till he's back in the deep.

Bo Rabbit chuckles and takes out his pocket knife.

Directly Whale gets tired and Elephant goes back on the hill, Bo Rabbit slips out and cuts the rope in the middle, *sazip, sazip, sazip.*

Then he grabs the end of the rope tied to Elephant and runs after him.

"What you say now, Elephant?" he cries, dancing around him and waving the rope in the air. "What you say now? You're not in your bed, are you? I pulled you right out of it, didn't I? Didn't I?"

Elephant looks at the rope in Bo Rabbit's hand. "How do you do it, Bo Rabbit? Little as you are and big as I am, how do you do it?"

"I'm one able little man, Elephant. But I'm not too little, am I? Say I'm not too little or I'll jerk you right over my head and throw you in the sea and drown you for true."

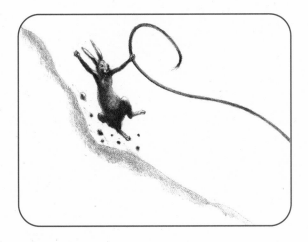

"You're not too little," Elephant is hasty to say.

"All right. You can go now."

"So long, Bo Rabbit. Maybe I get some sleep at last." Elephant lumbers off to bed.

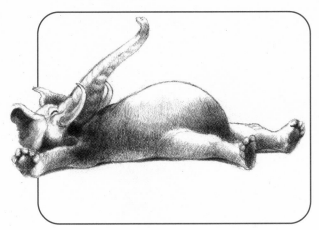

Bo Rabbit runs down the hill and picks up the end of the rope tied to Whale. Then he goes to the shore where Whale is waiting.

"What you say now, Whale?" he cries, dancing up and down and waving the rope in the air. "I pulled you clean out the deep, didn't I? Didn't I?"

Whale spouts, *Szi, Szi, Szi*, and looks at the rope in Bo Rabbit's hand. "How do you do it, Bo Rabbit? Little as you are and big as I am, how do you do it?"

"I'm one able little man, Whale. But I'm not too little, am I? Say I'm not too little or I jerk you right over my head and throw you up on the high hill."

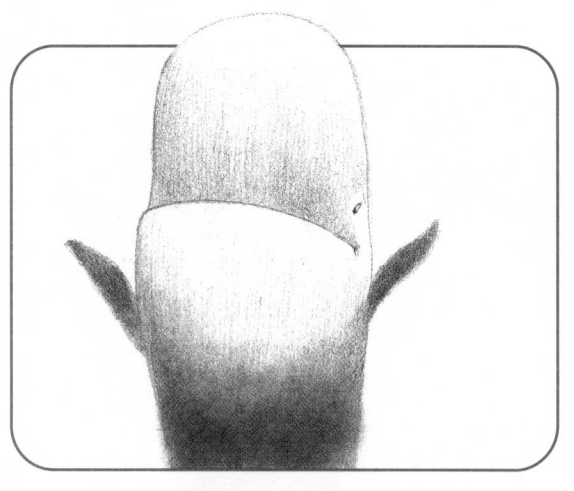

"You're not too little, Rabbit." Whale slaps the sea with his tail for emphasis, SPASHOW. "If you're any bigger, you can move the earth and flood the world and nobody be safe. Oh, no, you're not too little, Bo Rabbit. Not too little, at all."

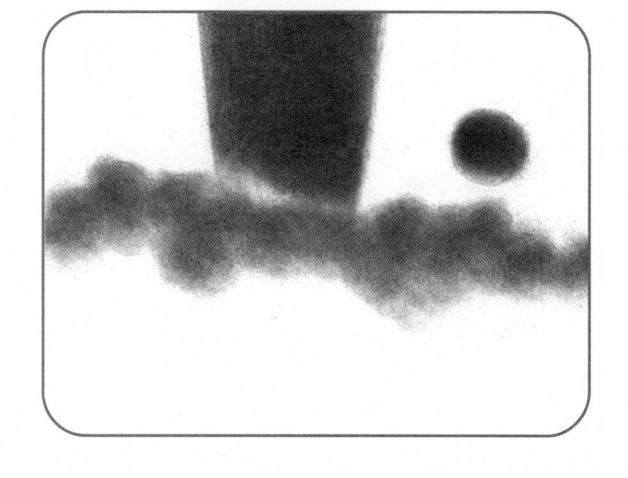

No matter how little you are, if you're smart for true, you can best the biggest crittuh in the sea and the biggest crittuh on earth. It stands so.

ALLIGATOR'S
SUNDAY SUIT

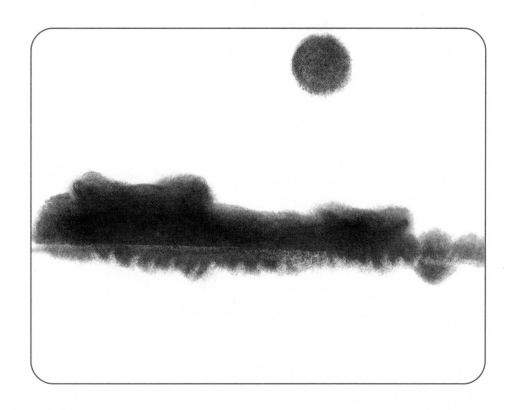

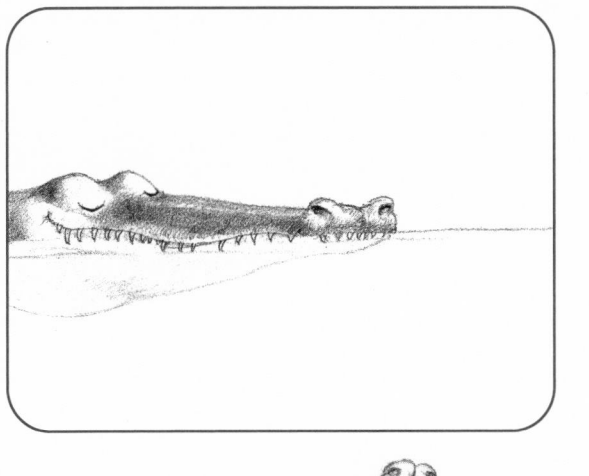

One day long ago, Alligator was floating in his home creek thinking how satisfy life is.

In those days, he's dress-up in a white suit good enough for Sunday all the time. He lives in the water with all the fish he can eat so he never has to work for a living. And he never, never meets up with trouble.

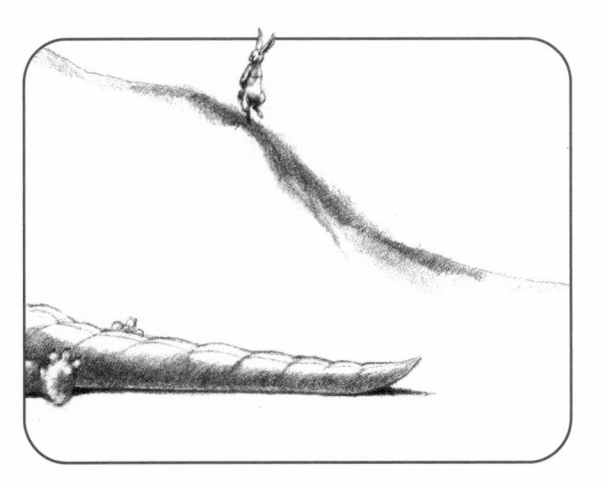

Well, Alligator is lazy in the sun-hot when here comes Bo Rabbit projecting along the creek shore.

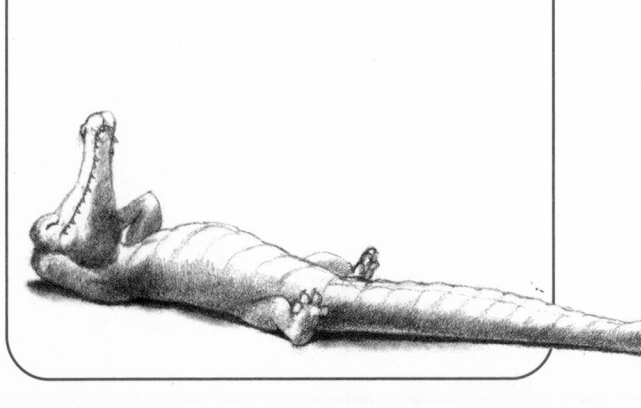

"G'morning, Alligator. How're you today?" asks Bo Rabbit, stopping to pass the time of day and other sociabilities.

"Doing just fine, thank you kindly. How's everyone to your house?"

"Oh, we making out. But so much trouble, Alligator. So much trouble."

"Trouble? What's that, Rabbit? I ain't never seen trouble."

"You ain't never seen trouble? Great Peace! I can show you trouble, Alligator."

"I'd like that, Bo Rabbit. I'd surely like to see how trouble stands."

"All right," Bo Rabbit makes response. "Meet me in the broomsage field tomorrow morning time the sun dries the dew off the grass good and I'll show you trouble."

Next morning time the sun gets high.

Alligator takes his hat and starts to leave the house. Miz Alligator asks him where he's going.

"I'm going to meet Bo Rabbit so he can show me how trouble stands."

"Well, if you're going to see trouble, I'm going, too."

"Hush up, you ain't going nowhere," says Alligator, high and mighty. "You best let me go see how trouble stands first. Then I can show you."

This makes Miz Alligator so mad she starts to arguefy.

They quarrel so loud till all the little alligators hear them and come sliding into the room, *hirr, hirr, hirr, hirr, hirr, hirr.*

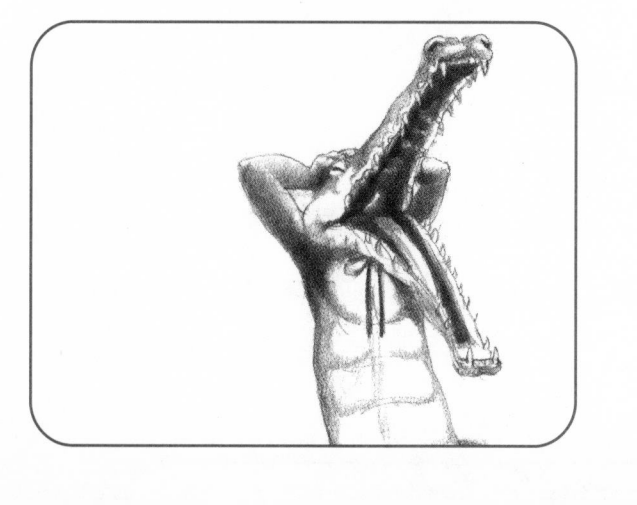

All the little alligators holler, "If you're going to see trouble, we're going, too. If you're going, we're going, too."

They make such a racket that to save his ears, Alligator roars, "Quiet! All right, all right. You *all* can come."

They cross the marsh and time they get in the broomsage field there's Bo Rabbit sitting on top a stump waiting for them.

"G'morning, Bo Rabbit," they say. And all the little alligators make their curtseys, *sazip, sazip, sazip, sazip, sazip, sazip.*

Bo Rabbit tells them "G'morning" back. "You all come to see trouble this morning, isn't it so?"

"It's so," says Alligator.

"It's so," say all the little alligators.

"All right. Stand out in the middle of the field and wait. I'll go get trouble and bring it."

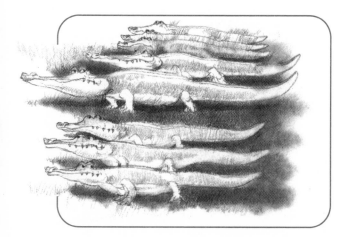

Alligator, Miz Alligator and all the little alligators slither into the field, KAPUK, *Kapuk, kapuk, kapuk, kapuk, kapuk, kapuk, kapuk.*

Bo Rabbit runs to the far edge and cuts him a hand of broomsage. Then he puts fire to it and runs it round and round the field till the fire runs round and round.

Miz Alligator sees the fire jumping up red and the smoke rising. "What's that yonder, Alligator?" She lives in the river and the wet marsh and never sees fire.

Alligator runs his eye around and shakes his head in puzzlement.

"I think that's the trouble Rabbit is bringing to show us," says Miz Alligator.

All the little alligators jump up and down and holler, "Ain't trouble pretty, Ma? Ain't trouble pretty?"

Soon the fire hot gets close and the smoke gets bad and all the alligators take out for one side of the field. They meet the fire.

They turn around to the other side. They meet the fire.

The fire gets so close it feels like it's going to burn them.

They all shut their eye and throw their head close to the ground and bust through the fire and never stop till, SPASHOW, Alligator jumps in the creek.

Right behind him, *Spashow*, Miz Alligator jumps in the creek.

Then all the little alligators come, *shu, shu, shu, shu, shu, shu*, in the creek.

As they scramble out, Bo Rabbit yells across the stream, "You've seen trouble now, Alligator. You like to see it again? I can show you."

"No, suh, Bo Rabbit. No, suh," says Alligator.

He looks at his suit. His white suit good enough for Sunday is gone.

He is blackish-green and rough and bumpy just the way he stands till yet.

"It's all Bo Rabbit's fault. Him and his Judas ways," says Alligator.

But even as the words come out his mouth, Alligator knows in his spirit that's not rightly so. He's the one asked to see trouble.

"I've learned one lesson for all my life," says Alligator. "Don't go looking for trouble, else you might find it."

COOTER'S
WING

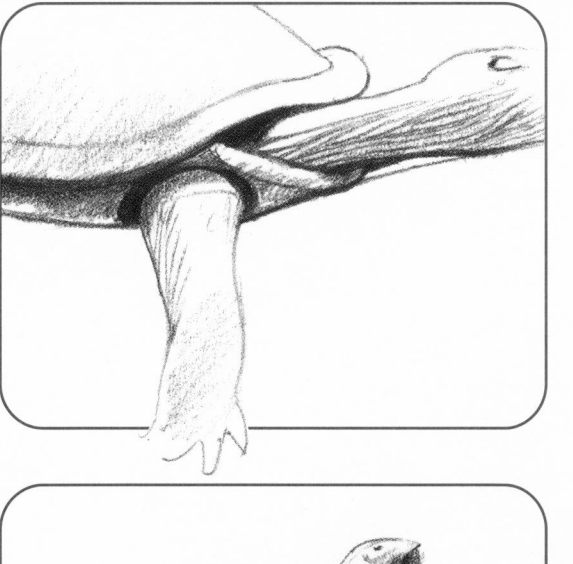

One middle-day long ago, Cooter was dozing in the sun-hot on his favorite log in the marsh when BIM BAM he hears Crow land on a stump nearby. Then, SHU SHU, Marsh Hen slides to a stop. Cooter opens his eye to see what brings them here and he sees Father standing tall.

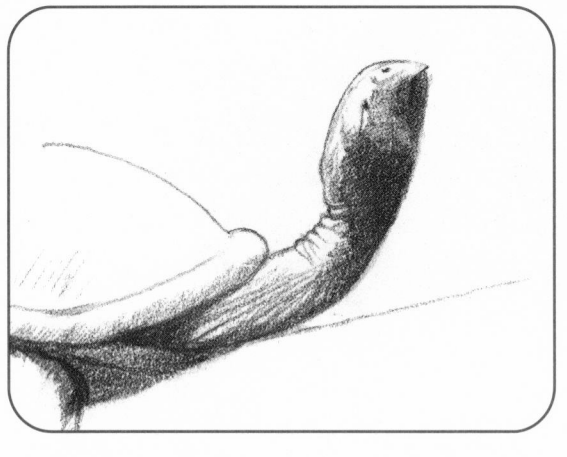

"This an invitation, Crow and Marsh Hen," Father say. "I want all the birds what have wing come up in Heaven next week Tuesday to one party I going to give. Hear?"

Cooter feels mighty sad. He wants to go to Heaven so bad for see how it stands but he looks at his shell. It is beautiful: smooth and white like a hen egg. But it has no wings.

Cooter lets out a sigh. "Well, one thing sure, if Father shares me short when he give out wings, he shares me long when he give out sense. Somehow I got to figure me a way to fly up in Heaven."

Directly Crane stalks by. "Hi, Po Jo, how're you today?" says Cooter.

Crane pulls in his long long neck and reconstructs himself for sociabilities. "Just fine, Cooter, thank you. How's everything to your house?"

"No complaints, Po Jo, no complaints. Only excepting I like to go to Father's party up in Heaven. You going, Po Jo?"

"I ain't been asked."

"You will be — this party for all the birds what have wing and can fly," says Cooter. "You so big and strong, Po Jo. When you do go up in Heaven, take me up in your foots with you, do. I surely want to see how Heaven stands before I dead and to dance one dance with them angel."

Po Jo heists his topknot in surprise. Then he shakes his head. "It's too far a distant for tote you up there, Cooter. I drop you for sure."

"You so strong you never drop me, Po Jo," says Cooter. But argue all he will, he can't change Crane's mind.

"I'll ask me another bird," says Cooter to himself and he starts to crawl out the marsh and down the big road, his leg so short he travels slow.

Middle-day passes and the sun lets down. Cooter travels on. But all the birds he sees are wren, hummingbird and sparrow. He knows they can't tote him up in Heaven, they too little.

At last he hears a ruckus in a sweet gum tree and sees the feather fly, feather blue as the October sky after first frost.

"Blue Jay in trouble," Cooter says to himself. "He tries to thief the sparrows' egg and they catch him. Time he gets away, I'll ask him will he take me up in Heaven."

Blue Jay swoops past, the sparrows dart at him, *kazip, kazip, kazip*. He circles back, the sparrows making darts, *kazip, kazip, kazip*.

Directly they stop, he lights to rest on a nearby fence post.

"Hey, Blue Jay," hollers Cooter.

"What you got on your mind, Cooter?"

"I want to go to Father's party so bad, Blue Jay. When you do go up in Heaven, take me up there with you, do. I surely want to see how Heaven stands before I dead and to dance one dance with them angel."

Blue Jay stretches his wing till the feather sparkle blue like the river when the breeze pass by.

Then he shakes his head. "It's too far a distant for tote you up there, Cooter. I drop you for sure."

"You so strong you never drop me," Cooter says. But all he argue, he can't change Blue Jay's mind.

Cooter peruses on down the road.

He asks every bird he meets — red bird, buzzard, yellowhammer — but they all tell him the same, they won't take him up in Heaven.

Time it's almost sundown Cooter comes to a cornfield and sees blackbirds all up and down the rows catching their last bite till morning.

"Hey, Blackbird," he yells to the nearest one. "Whole gang of you is going up in Heaven to Father's party, isn't it so?"

"It's so, Cooter."

"Blackbird, I want to go to Father's party so bad. Enough of you can get around me for take me up and when they tire, some of the other rest can take their place.

"I surely want to see how Heaven stands before I dead and to dance one dance with them angel. Take me up with you, do."

Blackbird shakes his head. "We ain't take you up in no Heaven, Cooter. You ain't no business for go up there."

Grieving in his spirit, Cooter starts home.

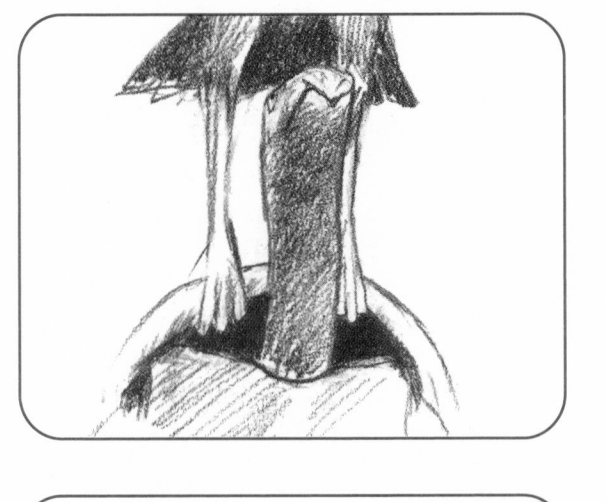

One day before the party Crow comes in the marsh for catch fish. Cooter makes up his mind for try one time more.

"Crow," he says. "You so big and strong. When you going to Father's party, take me up in your foots and take me up there, do."

Crow knows he won't take Cooter up in Heaven but he so loves to jook people, he says, "Yeh, yeh, yeh. Be ready soon in the morning, Cooter. I take you up."

Next day at sun up, Crow comes to Cooter's house. He calls, "You ready, Cooter?"

Cooter comes out, his shell all smooth and white and polished for the party.

Crow hooks all two his foots underneath Cooter's shell and take him up in the air.

Time they get up a good little piece, Crow says, "I hope my foots don't slip their hold, Cooter."

Cooter looks down, way, way down on the marsh, green and brown and little.

He feels squeamish in his soul and he knows Blackbird is right — he has no business going up in Heaven.

He cries out, "Do, Crow, if your foots going to slip their hold, take me back on the ground before you drop me from way up here."

"I think I can make it, Cooter." And Crow keeps going up.

Time he gets way up in the air, he sort of loose one of his foots easy and he hollers, "I do lose my hold. What I for do?"

Before Cooter can say anything, Crow opens the other of his foots and Cooter starts to fall and turns over and over, *fahlip, fahlip, fahlip*.

Crow makes darts at him and hollers, "Stop turning, Cooter, so I can catch you. Stop turning."

Crow knows Cooter can't stop but he keeps making darts at him, *kazip, kazip, kazip*, like he try for catch him.

Faster and faster Cooter goes sumbleset towards the ground.

SPASHOW, he lands flat on his back in the marsh.

Soon as Crow sees that, he laughs *haw, haw, haw* and flaps off.

Cooter is that deep in the marsh till he most can't get out. He fights and fights. Finally, at last, he gets loose.

He comes fine out of his fall. But when he gets home and washes off his shell, his beautiful shell, smooth and white like a hen egg, is gone.

He falls so hard the marsh mud goes in the shell and makes him yellowish and where the shell cracks up, the mud goes so deep, they's almost black.

From that day till yet, Cooter has these exact same markings.

Every time he looks at them, he knows he has one lesson hammered home hard: Don't try for do something you've no business doing.

Crittuh without wings belong on earth. Be satisfy with what Father give you and enjoy.

BO RABBIT'S
HIDE-AND-SEEK

One evening at sun-cool Bo Rabbit was pleasuring himself in the meadow

when he sees Eagle's speck in the sky

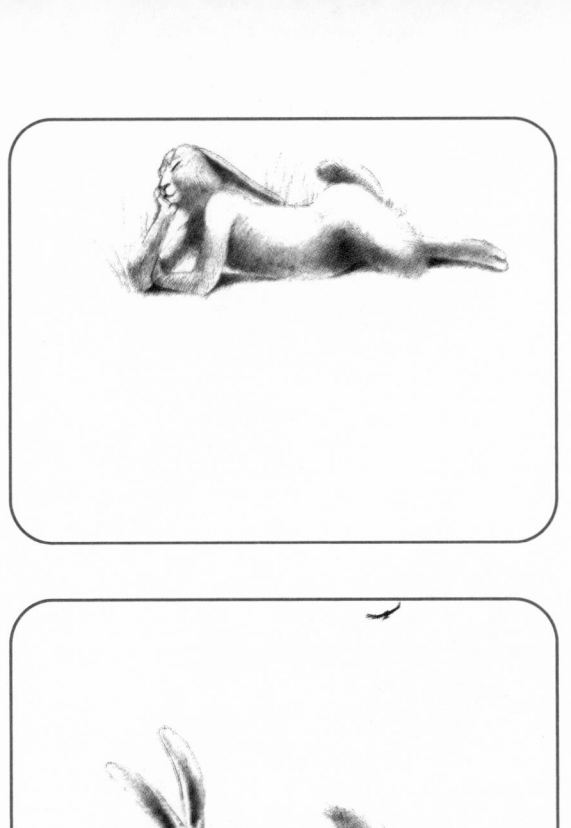

grow big as a sandfly and then big as a sparrow.

Before Eagle can fall on him,

SWOOSH,

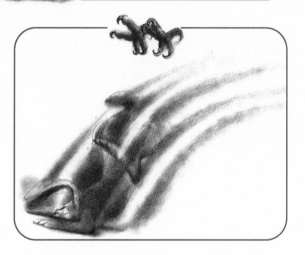

Bo Rabbit takes his foot in his hand and runs till he tumbles into the bramble patch.

Eagle swoops by and then climbs into the sky until he's only a speck again.

"That was close, Rabbit," says a voice from the clearing nearby.

Bo Rabbit looks. He can't see anyone. Then Partridge steps out, KIPIT.

Behind him comes Miz Partridge, *Kipit.* And behind her, all the little partridges, *kipit, kipit, kipit...*

"Evening, Miz Partridge. Been a long time, Partridge, since I see you," says Bo Rabbit. "Long enough for you to start a family, I see.

"And a mighty handsome family, too. Mighty handsome."

"Thank you kindly, Rabbit." Partridge stops abruptly, PIDUK. Miz Partridge stops fast, *Piduk,* and all the little partridges stop, bumping into each other, *piduk, piduk, piduk...*

Partridge looks fondly at them. "Such a handful. So unmannersable." He shakes his head. "So hard to bring young ones up right today, Rabbit, isn't it so?"

Miz Partridge nods agreement and Bo Rabbit scratches his head. "What kind of bringing up you have in mind, Partridge? You mean how to act or when to act? Like when Eagle swoops, you run fast?"

"Run?" Partridge was shocked. "Hide is the way to fool Eagle. Why, before these children can fly, Rabbit, they learn to hide."

"You're wrong to teach 'hide,' Partridge. 'Run' is what to teach," says Bo Rabbit. "Anyone can hide. Why, I can hide better than anyone in the world."

"*Tsip,*" chirps Miz Partridge in astonishment and "*tsip, tsip, tsip,*" cheep all the little partridges.

"Better than Dad?" says the littlest.

Partridge frowns on him. "Of course not. Rabbit knows nobody hides better than me."

"I surely don't know that, Partridge. I surely don't. Why, if I was to try, I could hide so nobody could find me."

"Go along, Rabbit. You always got so much to say for yourself."

"Show him, Dad. Show him you can hide better," cry all the little partridges hopping up and down, *ki, ki, ki...*

"I'll prove it to you, Partridge. Any time, any place you say."

"All right, Rabbit. Meet me in the clearing by the big log tomorrow at sun-up and I'll show you how to hide."

Next morning Bo Rabbit goes to the clearing. Partridge and his family are sitting on a log, waiting.

"Morning, Rabbit," says Partridge. "Here's the way for us to do.

"First you hide yourself and when you hide good, you *whoop*. When I hear you *whoop*, I'll go hunt you. Then it's my turn to hide."

"All right," says Bo Rabbit.

He goes into the brush and hides himself underneath a bush where nobody can see him. Then he *whoops*.

But when Bo Rabbit hides, he's so scared someone will come up on top of him and catch him and he won't see them coming that he keeps running his eye out of the bush so he can look all around.

When Partridge hears Bo Rabbit *whoop*, he starts hunting.

Miz Partridge stays comfortable on the log where she can keep an eye on the children. They are very mannersable and stay quiet, just watching.

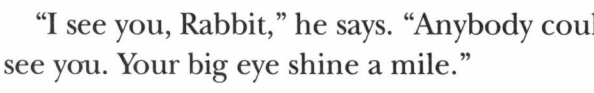

Partridge looks this way and that. Right away, he sees Bo Rabbit's big eye shine out of the bush.

"I see you, Rabbit," he says. "Anybody could see you. Your big eye shine a mile."

"Good for you, Dad. Good, good," cry all the little partridges hopping up and down, *ki, ki, ki...*

Now it's Partridge's turn. He tells Bo Rabbit the very exact spot he's going to hide himself. Then he goes down to that exact spot and hides.

And then he *whoops.*

When Bo Rabbit hears him *whoop,* he starts hunting. All the little partridges follow and watch.

Bo Rabbit goes to the exact spot and he doesn't see Partridge. He looks all about and he doesn't see Partridge.

He takes his hand and parts all the grass, yet he doesn't see Partridge.

He gets down on his hands and knees and he turns all the leaves and he searches all about, all about for a long time. He still doesn't see Partridge.

By and by, Bo Rabbit gets tired. He stands up on his feet. "Partridge, I give up."

"If you do, then move from on top of me so I can get up," says Partridge.

Bo Rabbit jumps aside and Partridge rises. Bo Rabbit looks at Partridge.

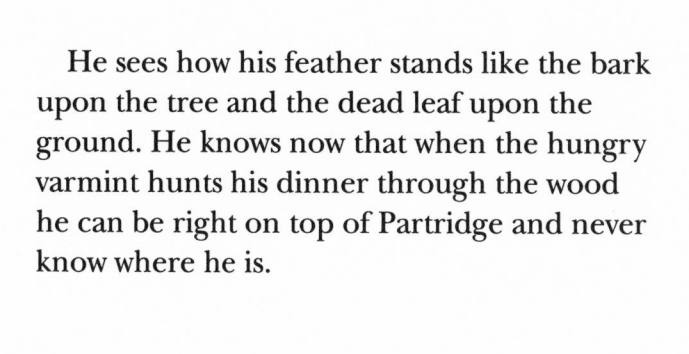

He sees how his feather stands like the bark upon the tree and the dead leaf upon the ground. He knows now that when the hungry varmint hunts his dinner through the wood he can be right on top of Partridge and never know where he is.

"You're right, Partridge," he says. "You're right to teach your children hide is best. You got the feather to hide. I got the long leg to run."

Miz Partridge hops down from the log and all the little partridges start jumping up and down cheeping, "You did it, Dad. You did it. You showed Rabbit how to hide."

"Children, behave," says Partridge. "There's no call to jubilate. Rabbit knows now what's right for some of us ain't necessarily right for others.

"We each got our own ways and we best accommodate ourselves and respect each other. Isn't it so, Rabbit?"

"Yes, suh, Partridge," says Bo Rabbit, "Yes, suh."

MANNERS
FOR TRUE

Crane was fishing. He stood in the creek and never moved till he saw a fish. Then, *tsip, tsip, tsip,* he stabbed it with his long beak and swallowed it down his long

   gll-umph   long
        gll-umph

throat.

He was taking his last gulp when Fox happens by.
   "Morning, Crane. Good fishing today?"
   "So-so, Fox. So-so."
   "Why not have dinner with me, Crane? Next Tuesday, say?"

Now you see, Crane is forever hungry. His stomach stands so far from his mouth that when the victual travels down his throat, before he's swallowed it good, his stomach rings the bell to tell his mouth dinner time has come again. So he says,
   "Thank you kindly, Fox. I'll be there sure as frog has foot!"

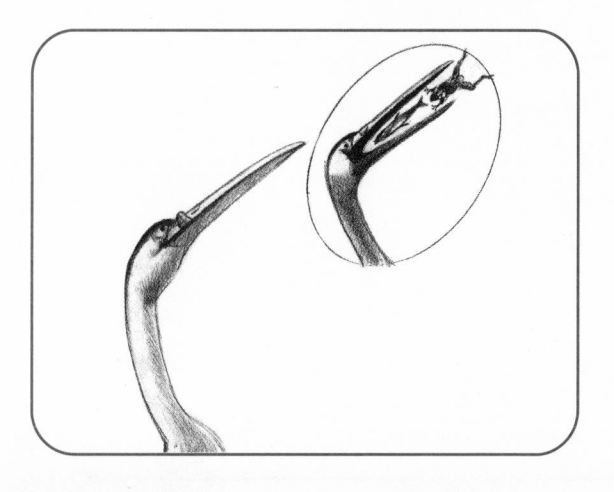

Tuesday all day Crane ponders what Fox will serve.
   "If Fox has good manners," he says to himself, "he'll have frog or even fish because he knows Crane loves those two.

And a mannersable man, when he asks someone to his house, tries to give him victuals he likes."

The more he thinks upon it, the more the hunger gnaws him. When he reaches Fox's house, he is that hasty to eat, he knocks upon the door, *bram, bram, bram,* loud as Woodpecker knocks on the pine tree.

Fox throws the door wide open and invites him in.

Soon as Crane smooths out his tail feathers and reconstructs himself, he heists his topknot just the way somebody heists his eyebrow to ask a question and looks down at Fox.

Now, Fox is smart and he knows very well that topknot is asking, "Isn't it time to eat?" So he says, "Crane, I've had my servant go to that very swamp where you fish every day and catch a heap of those big Granddaddy bullfrogs for a stylish frog soup. Let's eat."

It is frog soup for true but it's in a broad shallow dish which stands flat as a fannugh!

When Crane looks down on it, it makes his mouth water.

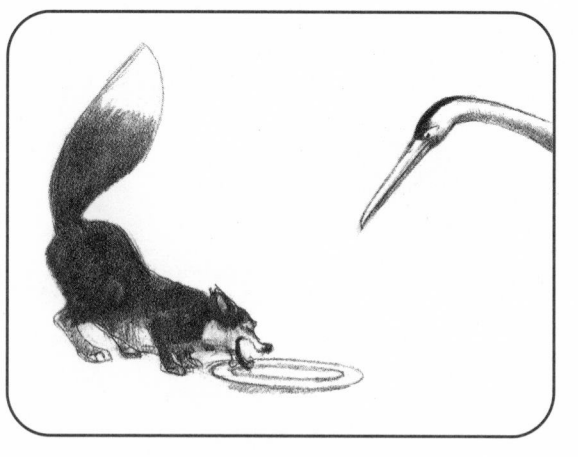

"Eat hearty, Crane. Eat hearty." Fox laps the soup up easy as a hound laps water from the branch, *sefu, sefu, sefu.*

But Crane's mouth isn't made for a plate. When he jams that long beak into it, he cannot get a drop. *Kurup, kurup, kurup,* he tries. When he sees his mouth cannot specify, he moves away.

Fox laps the soup all up, *sefu, sefu, sefu,* and grins like he's done something smart.

Crane makes his manners and goes. He flies till he reaches the swamp.

Then he takes his stand on the old dead log by the creek and he never stops eating frogs till sundown.

Two or three days later, he meets Fox in the path and says, "Fox, you've been so mannersable asking me to your house to eat, now you have to have dinner at my house, isn't that so?"

"Thank you, Crane," says Fox. "All you have to do is name the day."
"Come next Monday," says Crane.

All Monday Fox ponders what Crane will serve. "He's sure to have fish or 'possum for dinner because he knows Fox loves those two. And a mannersable man, when he asks someone to eat at his house, tries to give him victuals he likes."

Fox finally knocks on Crane's door. *Bam, bam, bam.*

"Come in, Fox," says Crane. "I've a treat for you. You love fish, I know. So I catch a big mess of fish in that same swamp you got the bullfrogs. Dinner is fixed. Time to eat!"

Dinner is fixed for true. But not for Fox. His mouth isn't made for a jar. Nothing but Crane's beak can get through that narrow neck!

"Help yourself, Fox." Crane never bothers about Fox again. He jams his long beak into the jar, stabs a piece of fish, and tilts it down his throat, *gll-umph, gll-umph, gll-umph.*

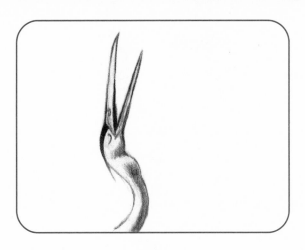

He picks that fish up piece by piece and every time he swallows one, Fox watches it as it goes down Crane's throat till by and by it travels all the way down and gets home.

Now and then Crane drops a piece. Fox snaps it up and swallows it quick.

Then Fox licks his tongue around the outside of his jaw to grease his mouth, *silop, silop, silop*.

But that's all the chance he gets to eat.

By and by Crane stabs the last piece and chokes it down and wipes his beak on his wing feathers.

"I'm glad you came, Fox," he says. "And I'm glad you had such a hearty appetite. Seems like you have really enjoyed your victuals."

Fox swells up with vexation till he almost chokes. Then he cools off and begins to laugh.

"I'm vexed no more, Crane," he says.

" 'Cause I've been a fool."

"At my house I thought it smart to eat while your belly pinched you. But now my own is gnawing me, I see I treated you very no-mannersable. You served me right."

It doesn't matter what a man's mouth says. If he has good manners for true, he has them in his heart and he'll never pinch anyone's belly and he'll never hurt anyone's feelings.

It stands so.

RATTLESNAKE'S WORD

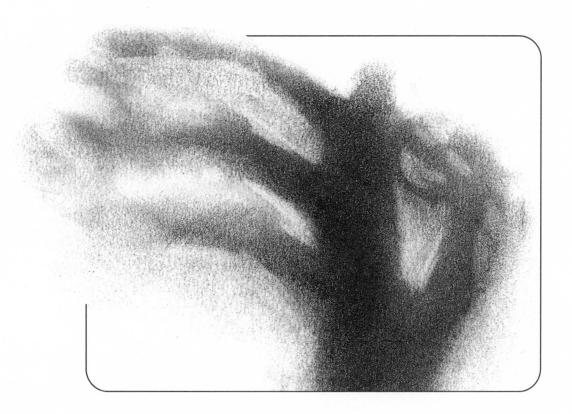

One windy day before sun-up Rattlesnake was slithering through the piney wood when BRAM a dead branch falls and pins him to the ground.

Rattlesnake is so vexed he sings his rattle, *Sssszzz, Sssszzz, Sssszzz.* Then he twists and coils to get out from under that branch. But twist and coil till he's tuckered out, he can't get free.

"I best wait till somebody comes by and lifts this log," he says to himself.

But nobody comes. Day-in-the-morning turns to day-clean. Still nobody comes.

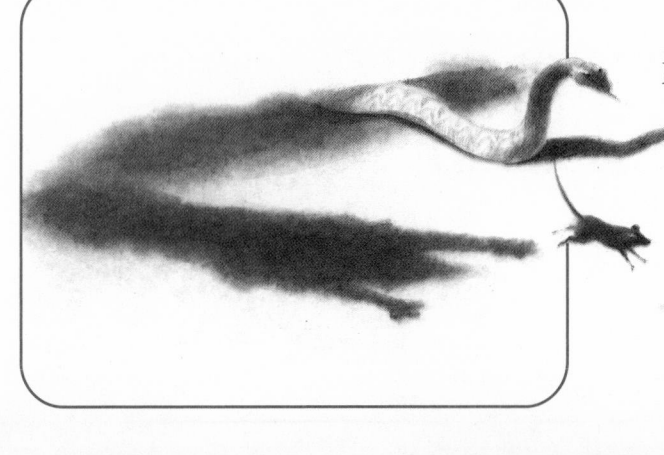

By and by, *skt, skt, skt,* a twig breaks. Rattlesnake turns his head.

Here comes Mouse running for his life and Fox after him.

Suddenly, *pufu, pufu, pufu,* Mouse pops down a hole and Fox pounces at air.

"Hi, Fox, I hope Mouse recognize his luck. You're the finest hunter in the wood, all the world knows that," says Rattlesnake, and makes a great admiration over him. "You steal up and drop on a crittuh so quick he never knows it till he's dead. You tote a mighty heavy game bag there, Fox, mighty heavy."

Fox combs his flank with his tongue. "I been after dinner all night, Rattlesnake. Hungry won't catch me for a while. But how come you get under that log?"

"Accident, Fox, accident. I'm minding my own business when BRAM this branch falls on me. Come, move it off of me, do, Fox. My back is hurting bad."

"Why would I do that?" asks Fox. "Once I do that, you charm me with your eye till I move close and then you bite me dead."

"Would I do that to a friend who helps me?" asks Rattlesnake. "Oh, no, Fox, I never do that."

Fox just grins. "You never bite me from under that log, that's for true."
He trots off.

Rattlesnake composes himself. Nobody comes. Day-clean turns to middle-of-the-day and he gets hot. Still nobody comes.

By and by, *bbzzz, bbzzz, bbzzz,* a bee flies past. After it comes Bear, his eye fast to watch it and his foot to follow.

"Hi, Bear," calls Rattlesnake.

Bear pays him no mind. He keeps going till he reaches a dead tree. He starts to climb it.

Halfway up, Bear stops and sticks his arm into a hole. Then he pulls out his hand and licks it.

"Bear found him a wild honey tree," says Rattlesnake to himself. "When he comes by again, happy from all that sweetness, he sets me free for sure."

Presently here comes Bear again, easy and slow, his mouth all sticky.

"Hi Bear," says Rattlesnake. "Mighty nice harvest you catch there. But all the crittuhs know you're the clever one to track down the wild bee and find the sweetest honey in the wood."

Bear licks his mouth. "It is sweet for true. But how come you get under that log, Rattlesnake?"

"Accident, Bear, accident. This branch blows down and BRAM it lands on top of me. Come move it off of me, Bear, do. My back is hurting bad."

"Why would I do that, Rattlesnake?" asks Bear. "If I do that, you charm me with your eye till I move close and then you bite me dead."

"Would I do that to a friend who helps me?" asks Rattlesnake. "Oh, no, Bear, I never do that."

"You promise?"

"I promise."

Bear lifts the log, *hrup, hrup, hrup.*

Before he can even turn his head, Rattlesnake fixes him with his cold eye and charms him till he can't move. Bear stands there all a-tremble and tries to hold himself from going closer and closer till he gets so close Rattlesnake can bite him dead.

Just then, *Scrr, Scrr, Scrr,* comes the scuffle of someone landing on a pile of dead leaves. Bear hears it and has just enough sense left to holler, "Help, whoever it is, help! help!"

"It's me, Bo Rabbit. What's wrong, Bear?"

"Nothing's wrong, Rabbit," says Rattlesnake. "Me and Bear just having a friendly little get-together is all."

"That so, Bear?"

"No, Rabbit." Bear tells him the truth. "Now Rattlesnake charms me and I can't move."

Bo Rabbit hops over to the log and studies it. "You never been caught under there, Rattlesnake. I don't believe it."

"You're wrong, Rabbit. I surely was fasten under that log."

"The one end of the log is heisted on that rock. You got room for you and half your family under there."

Rattlesnake darts a look. "Oh, that's not where the log was, Rabbit. When Bear lifts it off of me, he throws it off aways."

"Rattlesnake, I never believe you caught under that log till I see with my own eyes where it was."

"You don't believe me? You calling me a liar?" Rattlesnake is getting vexed. "Bear, bring that log back."

Bear brings it back, *hrup, hrup, hrup.*

Bo Rabbit hops around and around it. "It's flat to the ground, Rattlesnake. You never been under there. You're too fat to get under."

Rattlesnake is that vain about his figure, his long, slim figure, that he rises up in rage.

"Fat? Me too fat?" He sings his rattle, *Sssszzz, Sssszzz, Sssszzz.* "You call me fat, Rabbit. And you call me a liar. Bear, lift up that log. I show you, Rabbit."

Bear lifts the log, *hrup, hrup, hrup* and Rattlesnake slides under.

Bo Rabbit whispers, "Drop it, Bear, drop it!"

Bear drops the log and pins Rattlesnake to the ground once more. He sings his rattle again in fury, *Sssszzz, Sssszzz, Sssszzz.* Then he twists and coils to get out but he can't. He's caught tight.

"Thank you, Rabbit, thank you kindly," says Bear as they set off through the wood.

"Glad to oblige, Bear. Just goes to show you got to study who says a thing before you take it for true. A man's word is no better than the man himself. It stands so."

Notes

Some of the Gullah tales, like most folktales, trace their roots to far countries and are centuries old. Others seem to have originated long ago in the southern United States. Scholars think many reached Europe from India and were then carried to Africa by Portuguese, Spanish, and Dutch sailors. From there, they were brought to the Americas, sometimes by Africans, sometimes by voyagers from Europe.

Bo Rabbit Smart for True: In 1893, Professor Adolph Gerber reported an almost exact duplication of this tale from the island of Mauritius, in the Indian Ocean. Hare is the hero instead of Rabbit, and he challenges Elephant and Whale and wins by tying them together. Herbert H. Smith reported a variant from Brazil in 1879, in which a tortoise outwits a tapir and pulls him into the sea.

Alligator's Sunday Suit: Several versions of this tale have been reported from the South. In 1888, Charles C. Jones, Jr., in his *Negro Myths from the Georgia Coast,* told how Rabbit, learning that Alligator has never seen trouble, waits until he falls asleep in the broomsage and then sets it on fire around him. In 1892, Mrs. A. M. H. Christensen reported a version from the Sea Islands of South Carolina, in which Alligator asks to see trouble and Rabbit tells him to go to the broomsage field when the wind is blowing from the "Norderwest." Elsie Clews Parsons recorded in 1917 (*Journal of American Folk-lore*) a tale from Guilford County, North Carolina, about a terrapin in a brush-heap who volunteers to keep Rabbit company on a walk. When Rabbit finds Terrapin can't keep up, he sets the brush-heap on fire. "'I reckon you'll run now.'" Joel Chandler Harris told a version of "Alligator's Sunday Suit" in which Rabbit, running for his life from a dog, happens on Alligator, who laughs at Rabbit's plight and then crawls into the broomsage for a nap, whereupon Rabbit fires the grass and introduces him to trouble.

Cooter's Wing: Variants of this tale occur in many cultures from the Lesser Antilles, Jamaica, the Cape Verde Islands, and among the Ashanti, the Zuni, the Hopi, and the Uinta Ute.

In the Trinidad version, God gives a breakfast for the birds and Tortoise wants to go so badly that he asks every bird for a feather. They agree, and all fly to Paradise. But when they sit down to eat, Tortoise spreads his flappers around the table and eats all the food himself. The birds are so angry they take back their feathers and Tortoise falls to the earth.

In a similar version from Guadeloupe, God comes to Tortoise's help after the birds take back their feathers and lets him down on a cord. But Eagle sees him falling and cuts the cord. Tortoise falls to earth and is smashed to bits. God pieces him together, and that's why Tortoise's shell looks the way it does today—a patchwork of tiny pieces.

Bo Rabbit's Hide-and-Seek: Elsie Clews Parsons (*Memoirs of the American Folk-lore Society,* 1923) reports a variant of this story from Hilton Head, one of the Sea Islands off South Carolina. Partridge bets Rabbit he can hide in a patch of broomsage so well that Rabbit can't find him. Rabbit, sure he'll win the bet, agrees to give Partridge one of his children if he fails. Rabbit hunts and hunts. Then, convinced Partridge can't be there, Rabbit sets the grass on fire. Partridge, having won the bet, flies up and goes home, taking a rabbit child.

Manners for True: Although literary fables rarely surface in oral folktales, this is a typical example of one that does. Originally it appeared in *Aesop's Fables* as "The Fox and the Stork."

The same characters are used in Brazil, the Cape Verde Islands, and on St. Kitts, one of the Lesser Antilles. Although the moral remains the same as in the Gullah version, it is expressed less directly. "Oh, Fox," says Stork in the St. Kitts tale, "what joke you don't like for yourself, don't give to another man." The Gullah simply called such conduct "unmannersable."

Rattlesnake's Word: So widespread is this story that in "The Folk Tale," Stith Thompson called it "Type 155," "Ungrateful Serpent Returned to Captivity." Perhaps the oldest authenticated variant stems from tales about Reynard the Fox which circulated in the Middle Ages on the Flemish border, and were first written down in the twelfth century in Latin, German, and French. A Flemish version includes the story of a man who rescues a snake from a snare when the snake promises not to injure him. Once the snake is released, it threatens him, however, and the man appeals to a raven, a bear, and a wolf, who all refuse to condemn the snake. Finally the man seeks arbitration from a fox. Substitute Bo Rabbit for the fox and Bear for the man and you have this Gullah tale.

Even more similar to "Rattlesnake's Word" is this version from the Hottentots of South Africa, reported by W. H. I. Bleek in 1864: A man rescues Snake from under a rock and then is himself rescued by Jackal, who insists he won't believe Snake was under a rock until he sees it with his own two eyes.

From Mexico comes a story reported by Franz Boas in 1912 (*Journal of American Folk-lore*), of a rabbit rescuing a serpent from under a stone and asking a horse, a steer, and a donkey for help. After they all refuse, a rooster steps in to save the rabbit.

According to Herbert H. Smith, writing in 1879, Tupi Indians along the Amazon tell another variant, in which a fox or an opossum finds a jaguar stuck in a hole. Once released, the jaguar threatens to eat the fox. A wise man passing by saves the fox by tricking the jaguar into going back in the hole.

Bibliography

Aesop's Fables, compiled by Russell Ashe and Bernard Higton. San Francisco: Chronicle Books, 1990.

W. R. Bascom. "Acculturation Among the Gullah Negroes," *American Anthropologist,* 43 (1941): 43–50.

John Bennett. "Gullah, a Negro Patois," *The South Atlantic Quarterly,* October 1908: Part I, 332–347; Part II, 39–52.

W. H. I. Bleek. *Reynard, the Fox, in South Africa; or Hottentot Fables and Tales.* London: T. Rubner and Company, 1864.

Franz Boas. "Notes on Mexican Folklore," *Journal of American Folk-lore,* 25 (1912): 204–260.

Stella Brewer Brookes. *Joel Chandler Harris, Folklorist.* Athens: University of Georgia Press, 1950.

Mrs. A. M. H. Christensen. *Afro-American Folklore Told Round Cabin Fires on the Sea Islands of South Carolina.* Boston: J. G. Cupples, 1892.

T. F. Crane. "Review of Cosquin's *Contes Populaires de Lorraine,"* *Modern Language Notes,* 2 (April 1887): 87–91.

Mason Crum. *Gullah: Negro Life in the Carolina Sea Isles.* Durham, NC: Duke University Press, 1940.

Duncan Emrich. *Folklore on the American Land.* Boston: Little, Brown, 1972.

William J. Faulkner. *The Days When the Animals Talked: Black American Folktales and How They Came to Be.* Chicago: Follett Publishing, 1977.

Adolph Gerber. "Uncle Remus Traced to the Old World," *Journal of American Folk-lore,* 6 (1893): 245–247.

Ambrose E. Gonzales. *The Black Border: Gullah Stories of the Carolina Coast.* Columbia, SC: The State Co., 1922.

———. *The Captain: Stories of the Black Border.* Columbia, SC: The State Co., 1924.

———. *Laguerre, a Gascon of the Black Border.* Columbia, SC: The State Co., 1924.

———. *With Aesop Along the Black Border.* Columbia, SC: The State Co., 1924.

Joel Chandler Harris. *Nights with Uncle Remus.* Boston and New York: Houghton Mifflin, 1911.

———. *Uncle Remus: His Songs and His Sayings.* Boston and New York: Houghton Mifflin, 1915.

Charles F. Hartt. *Amazonian Tortoise Myths.* Rio de Janeiro: William Scully, 1875.

Guy B. Johnson. *Folk Culture on St. Helena Island, South Carolina.* Hatboro, PA: Folklore Associates, 1968 (reprint of the 1930 edition published by the University of North Carolina Press).

Charles Colcock Jones, Jr. *Negro Myths from the Georgia Coast, Told in the Vernacular.* Boston and New York: Houghton Mifflin, 1888.

Ernest Martin. *Le Roman de Renart.* Strasbourg and Paris, 1882.

Elsie Clews Parsons. *Folklore of the Antilles, French and English,* Part II. Cambridge, MA: American
        Folk-lore Society, 1926 *(Memoirs of the American Folk-lore Society, 26).*

————. *Folk-lore of the Antilles, French and English,* Part III. Cambridge, MA: American
        Folk-lore Society, 1943. *(Memoirs of the American Folk-lore Society, 26).*

————. *Folk-lore of the Sea Islands, South Carolina.* Cambridge, MA: American Folk-lore
        Society, 1923. (*Memoirs of the American Folk-lore Society,* 16).

————. "Tales from Guilford County, North Carolina," *Journal of American Folk-lore,* 30
        (1917): 179.

Herbert H. Smith. *Brazil: The Amazons and the Coast.* S. Low, Marston, Searle and Rivington,
        1879.

Reed Smith. *Gullah: Dedicated to the Memory of Ambrose E. Gonzales.* Columbia, SC: University of
        South Carolina Bureau of Publications, 1926 (*Bulletin of the University of South Carolina,*
        190 [November 1927]).

Sadie H. Stewart. "Seven Folk-Tales from the Sea Islands, South Carolina," *Journal of American
        Folk-lore,* 32 (1919): 394–396.

Albert H. Stoddard. *Animal Tales Told in the Gullah Dialect.* Washington, D.C.: Library of
        Congress, Archive of Folk Song Recordings, 1949.

Stith Thompson. *The Folktale.* New York: The Dryden Press, 1946.

Lorenzo Dow Turner. *Africanisms in the Gullah Dialect.* Chicago: University of Chicago Press,
        1949.

F. M. Warren. "Uncle Remus and the Roman de Renaud," *Modern Language Notes,* 4
        (May 1890): 129–135.

Marcellus S. Whaley. *The Old Types Pass: Gullah Sketches of the Carolina Sea Islands.* Boston:
        Christopher Publishing House, 1925.